9/10

Judy Moody & Stink

THE MAD, MAD, MAD, MAD TREASURE HUNT

Books about Judy Moody and Stink
by Megan McDonald, illustrated by Peter H. Reynolds:

Judy Moody & Stink: The Holly Joliday
Judy Moody
Judy Moody Gets Famous!
Judy Moody Saves the World!
Judy Moody Predicts the Future
Judy Moody, M.D.: The Doctor Is In!
Judy Moody Declares Independence
Judy Moody Around the World in 8½ Days
Judy Moody Goes to College
Stink: The Incredible Shrinking Kid
Stink and the Incredible Super-Galactic Jawbreaker
Stink and the World's Worst Super-Stinky Sneakers
Stink and the Great Guinea Pig Express
The Judy Moody Mood Journal
Judy Moody's Double-Rare Way-Not-Boring Book of Fun Stuff to Do

Other Candlewick Press books by Megan McDonald:
Ant and Honey Bee: What a Pair!
The Sisters Club

Other Candlewick Press books
written and illustrated by Peter H. Reynolds:
The Dot
Ish
The North Star
So Few of Me

Judy Moody & Stink

THE MAD, MAD, MAD, MAD TREASURE HUNT

Megan McDonald
illustrated by Peter H. Reynolds

CANDLEWICK PRESS

Text copyright © 2009 by Megan McDonald
Illustrations copyright © 2009 by Peter H. Reynolds
Judy Moody font copyright © 2004 by Peter H. Reynolds

Judy Moody®. Judy Moody is a registered trademark of Candlewick Press, Inc.

First paperback edition 2010

The Library of Congress has cataloged the hardcover edition as follows:

McDonald, Megan.
Judy Moody & Stink : the mad, mad, mad, mad treasure hunt / Megan McDonald ;
illustrated by Peter H. Reynolds. — 1st ed.
p. cm.
Summary: During a weekend trip to Ocracoke Island, Judy and Stink Moody take
part in a pirate treasure-hunting game, in which various clues lead them to silver coins,
or "pieces of eight," hidden across the island.
ISBN 978-0-7636-3962-4 (hardcover)
[1. Brothers and sisters—Fiction. 2. Treasure hunt (Game)—Fiction.
3. Pirates—Fiction. 4. Ocracoke Island (N.C.)—Fiction.] I. Reynolds, Peter, date, ill. II. Title. III.
Title: Judy Moody and Stink. IV. Title: Mad, mad, mad, mad treasure hunt.
PZ7.M478419Jual 2009
[Fic]—dc22   2008021533
ISBN 978-0-7636-4351-5 (paperback)
09 10 11 12 13 14 TWPS 10 9 8 7 6 5 4 3 2 1
Printed in Singapore

This book was typeset in Stone Informal and Judy Moody.
The illustrations were created digitally.

Candlewick Press
99 Dover Street
Somerville, Massachusetts 02144

visit us at www.candlewick.com

For Eliza
M. M.

For Holly McGhee
P. H. R.

CONTENTS

As long as ships have sailed the seas, there have been pirates. And as long as there have been pirates, Stink Moody has wanted to sail on a ship to an island. A *treasure* island.

A ferryboat wasn't exactly a pirate ship—but still! Stink reached into his survival kit (aka his backpack). Compass, flashlight, small notebook, *Treasure Island*, pirate flag, pirate rule book . . . spyglass!

From the upper deck of the ferry, Stink peered through his spyglass with one eye.

The eye not covered with a pirate patch, that is.

All he could see was blue, blue, blue. Blue sky. Blue water. Blue . . . T-shirt? His sister, Judy Moody, was blocking his view. "Hey, Judy. You make a better door than a window."

When Judy moved, Stink focused his spyglass on the horizon. "I think I see it," said Stink. "Vegetable Island! I mean, Artichoke Island."

"You mean Ocracoke Island," Judy corrected him.

"Whatever," said Stink. "I just want to meet pirates and look at shipwrecks and see real gold and find treasure."

"Yeah, right. We're only in North Carolina for a few days."

Through his spyglass, Stink spotted Mom and Dad down on the lower deck. "Ahoy! You there, on the poop deck," he called.

"What's the poop deck? Wait, that's where all the seagulls poop, right? Let me look." Judy grabbed the spyglass from Stink.

Stink swung his arms in the air and sang like a pirate:

"Fifteen men on the dead man's chest—
Yo-ho-ho, and a bucket of fun!"

"Hey, Stink, there's a boy on the poop deck staring up at you. That tall one wearing the turtle T-shirt. Next to that girl with the glasses. She looks smart. And she's staring at you, too."

Stink sliced the air with his invisible sword.

"Fifteen chests on the dead man's bum—
Yo-ho-ho, and a packet of gum!"

Stink pretended to walk the plank on the upper deck. The boat hit a bunch of waves. Judy hung on tight to the rail. Stink slumped to the deck, making pukey stomachache faces.

"What's wrong?" Judy asked. "Are you going to puke?"

"Arrrr! Never say 'puke' when a pirate's about to puke."

Judy tried to think of something—anything to take Stink's mind off the pukes. A joke! "Stink. What do you call pirate throw-up?"

"I said please DON'T say 'puke.' "

"I didn't say 'puke.' I said 'throw-up.' "

"You're like the Girl Who Cried Throw-Up or something."

"Okay, then what do you call pirate heave-ho?" said Judy.

"I call it *gross*," said Stink.

"No, you call it Pieces-o'-Ate!" She laughed herself silly.

"My feet itch." Stink scratched his feet like mad. "And my teeth hurt. Do I have red blotches on me? Are my teeth falling out?"

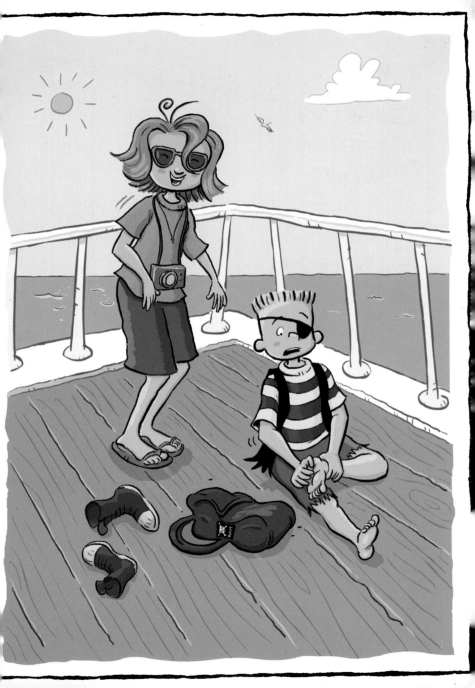

"Stick out your tongue and say *ARRRR*," said Doctor Judy. "Stink, you're already missing two teeth, and your face is sunburned."

"Tummy ache. Feet itch. Teeth falling out. Red face. *And* I'm cranky."

"I'll say."

"That's it. I have it."

"Have what?"

"Scurvy!" said Stink. "I'm dead."

"Scurvy!" said Judy. "You're just a little seasick. Close your eyes for a minute, and put your head between your knees. Here, Mom gave me crackers in case we felt like we might hurl."

Stink was quiet for a while, munching on crackers. Finally, when the boat wasn't

8

rocking anymore, he stood up. "I'm okay now. I feel much better." Stink even waved his red Jolly Roger at his parents.

"What's with the red pirate flag, Stink?" Judy asked.

"For your information, this was the flag of a real Moody pirate."

"A moody pirate? Rare! But weren't all pirates pretty grumpy?"

"His name was Christopher Moody," said Stink. "He sailed around the Carolinas with Black Bart. He's one of the only pirates with a red flag. It had a skull and crossbones, an arm with a dagger, and an hourglass with wings. That means, *Your time is running out.* Get it?"

"Whoa," said Judy. "A for-real pirate named Moody? Just think, Stink: Christopher Moody could be like our great-great-great-great-great-grandpa."

"Shiver me timbers!" yelled Stink.

"Rare!" said Judy. "I have pirate blood in me."

"Girls can't be pirates."

"Says who?"

"Says Pirate Rule Number Six: No girls allowed on ships. It's the Pirate Code." Stink pulled out the *Book of Pirate Rules.*

"See? There are ten pirate rules. Break one, and they feed you to the shark*sss.*"

"What about girl pirates like Anne Bonny and Mary Read, who dressed up like boys? Take that, Pirate Rule Number Six."

"Hey, don't be knocking the Pirate Rules."

"I read about a girl pirate who got her ear bitten off in a fight. She picked up her chewed-off ear and wore it on a chain around her neck. No lie."

Stink lifted up Judy's hair. "Looks to me like you still have both your ears," he said. "And the only thing around your neck is the shark-tooth necklace that I gave you."

"Avast, ye hairy carbuncle. Ye be spit on the scab of life, ye scurvy nuncle!"

Land, ho!" called Stink as the ferry pulled up to the dock. He ran down the gang-plank, singing like Captain Hook:

"Yo ho, yo ho, the frisky plank,
You walks along it so."

His legs felt all wibbly-wobbly.

"Still got yer sea legs on, I see," said a voice from the dock. A *scurvy* voice.

"Huh?" Stink looked up, squinting. A large shadow blotted out the sun. The shadow had a dirty kerchief and a scrag-gly beard. The shadow had an eye patch and a gold hoop earring.

The shadow was a pirate!

"Name's Cap'n Weevil," said the pirate. "But me friends call me Scurvy Sam."

"I think I had scurvy on the ferryboat!" said Stink.

"And who might ye be?"

"Um, Cap'n Moody, here," said Stink, pointing to himself.

"But his friends call him Scurvy Stink," Judy teased, coming up behind Stink.

"And this be Mad Molly O'Maggot." Stink pointed to Judy.

"Thanks a lot," Judy murmured.

"Welcome to Pirate Island," said Scurvy Sam, winking one eye.

"Pirate Island? I thought this was Okey Dokey Island," said Stink.

The pirate laughed. "Folks 'round here call it Pirate Island, on account o' Blackbeard himself haunted these parts back in the day."

"Whoa," said Stink. "Are you a for-real pirate? I mean, are ye?"

"O' course I'm real. Yank me beard if ye like, mate."

"Um, no thanks." *Pirate Rule Number Eleven: Do NOT get on the wrong side of a pirate, or he just might take your head off.*

"Get yer maps here," Scurvy Sam called to people getting off the ferry. He handed one to Judy.

"Listen up, all ye scumbuckets and scallywags," Scurvy Sam announced. "This be the weekend of the Third Annual

Pirate Island Treasure Hunt. Fun and mayhem start first thing in the morn."

"Really?" asked Stink.

"Really?" asked Judy.

"Would I lie t' ye?" asked the pirate.

"O' course," said Judy. "Yer a pirate."

"Ye got me there, lassie, but I'm not pulling yer leg this time. C'mon down to me pirate ship at Silver Lake Harbor. *X* marks the spot." He pointed to a big red *X* on the map. "I be givin' out the first clue to the treasure at ten hundred hours sharp. That'll give ye time to grub up and to catch forty winks before morn."

THIRD ANNUAL
PIRATE ISLAND
Treasure Hunt

OCRACOKE

Ye first clue be at me pirate ship

"What do we have to do?" Stink asked.

"Follow the trail of clues, laddie. First to collect sixteen pieces o' eight wins the gold doubloon."

"A doubloon is a gold coin," Stink told Judy. "It takes sixteen pieces of eight—silver dollars—to make one doubloon."

"I knew that," said Judy, even though she didn't.

"A pirate doubloon!" said Stink. "Is it real gold?"

"As gold as a pirate's tooth," Scurvy Sam joked. "If ye win, ye get a ride with me aboard Blackbeard's own pirate ship, the *Queen Anne's Revenge Two*. If ye dare."

"Sounds like a barrel o' fun," said Stink.

"'Taint easy," said Scurvy Sam. "Where there's pirates, there be tricks and tons of monkey business. *Yarr.*"

Dad walked up with their luggage. "C'mon. Time to get to the inn."

"And wash up before we grub up," said Mom, wheeling a suitcase.

"Did you hear?" said Stink. "A real treasure hunt. Right here on Pirate Island. Can we do it?"

"Can we, can we, can we?" asked Mad Molly and Scurvy Stink.

⚓ ⚓ ⚓

"Lights out at eight o'clock," Mom said when they got back to the Clam On Inn after supper. "That goes for flashlights, too. Pirate Rule Number Four."

"Not you, too!" Judy groaned. "It's vacation. Can't we stay up late? Bedtime isn't a pirate rule."

"No mutiny on the SS *Moody,*" Mom said, shaking her head.

Stink checked the pirate rule book. "She's right."

"C'mon, kids. We've had a long trip today," said Dad. "You'll want to have lots of energy for tomorrow's—"

"Treasure hunt!" screamed Judy and Stink at the same time.

Before they knew it, the two of them were catching forty winks.

Stink was the first one out of bed the next morning.

"Stink, you're wearing that striped pirate shirt again? Didn't you even take a bath?"

"Pirates don't take baths," said Stink. "Here, smell my armpit."

"Gross! You smell worse than a pirate's monkey on a poop deck!"

"*Yarr,*" said Stink.

After Mom and Dad woke up, drank buckets of coffee, and read the paper for a year, they took Judy and Stink to Silver Lake Harbor, where the treasure hunt was about to begin.

"I see it!" said Stink. "I see the pirate ship!"

Before them loomed the tall poles of the three-masted square-rigger, the *Queen Anne's Revenge II*. Sails flapped like kites in the wind. Kids and families gazed up at the ship in awe.

A ship's bell clanged several times in a row. Just then, a pirate swung down on a long rope from the yardarm (like Tarzan) and landed on deck with a loud *ker-PLUNK* (not like Tarzan). It was Scurvy Sam!

"Ahoy, ahoy, all ye treasure seekers," he called. "Welcome to the Third Annual

Pirate Island Treasure Hunt. Listen up, scallywags. There be five clues in all. Each clue'll lead ye to the next. When ye think ye figgered out a clue, turn it in to the nearest Assistant Pirate. They be wearin' a red sash and givin' out pieces o' eight. First one to figger out all five clues and turn in sixteen pieces o' eight wins the gold doubloon and a ride with me on the *QAR Two*."

Scurvy Sam held up a silver piece of eight. "I'll be givin' ye yer first piece o' eight. The last one is hidden, and it be harder to find than a bow tie on a pirate." Everybody laughed.

"If ye be the one to find it, make haste back to me at Pirate Headquarters. No wooden nickels allowed!" Scurvy Sam cackled. "One last thing—ye have until noon tomorrow. When ye hear the ship's bell, c'mon back to see if anybody won the gold. Everybody who joins in goes home with loot—a big bag o' pirate booty."

After a lot more *ahoys, avasts,* and *aye-ayes,* Scurvy Sam unrolled a parchment and read aloud the first clue for all to hear.

Clue 1

Tall as a tree,
dressed in white,
my bridal veil
is shiny bright.
Up all night,
never sleeping;
if I rest,
many are weeping.
Upon these shores
since days of old,
my silent message
points to gold.

"Good luck t' ye. May ye have strong winds at yer back, only bilge rats for enemies, and a barrel o' fun. Let the plunderin' begin!"

Judy and Stink said good-bye to Mom and Dad. "Dad and I are going to the beach. If we don't see you before noon, we'll meet you in front of Barnacle Bob's hot-dog stand at twelve thirty," Mom said.

"Have fun!" said Dad.

Stink and Judy pushed their way through the crowd, past the big bald man with a small boy on his shoulders, past the lady with three dogs, past the twin kids with Popsicles. When they got to the front, Scurvy Sam was handing out the first piece of eight and the first clue. A girl with braces stepped on Stink's foot while reaching for her coin.

"Stink, don't look now. It's Tall Boy and Smart Girl. The ones from the ferry yesterday." Judy cast a squinty-eyed look their way.

"Hurry up. Read the clue again," said Stink. "We have to beat them." They read the clue three times.

"Tall as a tree," said Stink. "It's gotta be the pirate ship. The masts are tall as a tree, and the sails could be the bride's thingie."

"It can't be the ship, Stink. Nobody's even allowed on the ship unless you win the gold."

"Then I think it's a flagpole. A flagpole is as tall as a tree."

"Well, I saw a church in the town, and it has a tall steeple. And it's white. A flagpole isn't dressed in white."

"It is if it's painted white," said Stink.

"Like the one I saw in front of the post office."

"But it doesn't have a bridal veil," said Judy.

"It does if it's flying a white flag," Stink said.

"All I know is that churches have brides."

Judy was right. Churches did have brides. *What a bilge rat.*

"And you could

say churches are up all night," said Judy. "You know, they're always open in case people need them."

"Flagpoles are up all night, too," said Stink.

"But they take the flag down at the end of the day."

"Scumbuckets!" Stink said. Judy was right again. "But what about the weeping? People cry when somebody dies, and the flag is put at half mast."

Stink had a point. "But people cry in churches, too," Judy said. "Like at a wedding. I say church."

"Flagpole," said Stink.

"Church."

"FLAGPOLE!"

"Hey! I call Pirate Rule Number Eight. No fighting," said Judy.

"That's only aboard ship," said Stink.

"I give in," said Judy. "Let's go to *both* places."

Judy craned her head back and squinted up at the flagpole outside the post office. "Stink, this flag isn't white."

"It's white *between* the red stripes," said Stink.

"Oh, brother. C'mon, let's go to the church," said Judy. But when they got to the church, it was locked.

"Aha! So it's *not* up all night," said Stink.

"At least it's tall and white and has brides," said Judy. But no Assistant Pirate with a sash was anywhere in sight.

"Think. What else is tall?" Stink looked up, down, and all around. He saw the lighthouse sticking out of the trees. "A lighthouse is tall!"

"And painted white!" said Judy.

"And it has a light that's shiny bright!" said Stink.

"And it's up all night!" said Judy. "And if it stops, ships will crash on the rocks."

"To the lighthouse!" said Stink, pointing the way.

⚓ ⚓ ⚓

The lighthouse stood tall, blinking in the sun. Stink squinted to read the plaque. "This lighthouse is so old."

"I know," said Judy.

36

"It's almost two hundred years old," said Stink.

"I know."

"This lighthouse is so tall," said Stink.

"I know."

"It's like seventy-five feet tall."

"I know."

"King Kong was only twenty-five feet tall."

"I know."

"You can see the light if you're fourteen miles away at sea."

"I know."

"They used to have to light it like a candlewick, in whale oil."

"I know."

"Every lighthouse has its own pattern of blinks, so ships will know where they are," said Stink.

"I—what?" Judy asked.

"Some even use Morse code. Didn't you know?" asked Stink.

"No, I didn't know lighthouses blinked

out a secret message in *Morse code*. Rare!" said Judy. "Stink, you're a genius."

"So how do we find the next clue?" Stink asked.

Judy wasn't listening. She was watching Tall Boy and Smart Girl talking to a park ranger. A park ranger wearing a pirate sash! "Let's go talk to that lady Assistant Pirate."

The park ranger had short curly hair and a Smokey-the-Bear hat. She smiled at Judy and Stink. "What's the password?" she whispered.

"Um . . . lighthouse?" they whispered at the same time.

"You just earned five pieces o' eight!"

Five! The ranger reached into a bucket and poured coins into Stink's hands. They jingled all the way.

Stink dug into his backpack, pulled out a shiny red pouch, and tied it to his belt. "This'll be for all our pirate booty. We have six already!"

"Ye better guard that booty with your life," said the ranger. "There be pirates all over these parts!" Then she handed them the next clue.

Judy and Stink sat on a driftwood log and opened the clue.

-... .-.. .- -.-. -.- -... . .- .-. -..

"It's in Morse code!" said Stink.

"Morse code? Oh, no! We don't have a clue what this means."

"Who says?" Stink reached into his survival backpack again.

"*Shh!*" said Judy. "Spies on deck. Spies on deck."

"You have the map," they heard Tall Boy tell Smart Girl. "Where's the library?"

"The library!" Judy whispered. "Good idea. Let's go—"

Stink held up a spiral notebook with Morse code on the cover.

"You have Morse code in your survival kit?" Judy asked.

"You never know when you might get marooned on a desert island, like Gilligan's Island, and have to send out a rescue signal."

"Stink, have I told you lately you're a genius?"

Stink grinned. "You just did. But tell me again."

Judy looked up each letter of the coded message, writing them down in Stink's notebook as she found them.

"What is it? What does it say?" Stink pestered.

"Let me finish," said Judy.

"It's *Bad-Bear*," said Stink. *"Blab-ear? Blackbird? Blackbear?"*

"BLACKBEARD!" screamed Judy and Stink at the same time, forgetting all about spies.

Judy and Stink met Mom and Dad in front of Barnacle Bob's. "Those two girls with painted faces have maps, too," said Judy, pointing.

"So does that surfer-dude kid," said Stink. "And *he's* not stopping to eat hot dogs."

Judy and Stink wolfed down hot dogs, then their parents drove them all over town while they tried to solve the next clue. Something about Blackbeard.

They went to Blackbeard's Castle.

They peeked inside a gift shop called Blackbeard's Folly. They checked out the Barefoot Blackbeard, a surf shop. But all they found were a lot of flip-flops.

"Let's park and walk into the center of town," said Mom. "I need to get sunscreen. And I'm hoping to find some art supplies so we—"

"Do we have to?" asked Stink. He could already feel his feet falling off from all the boring old shopping.

"C'mon—it'll be fun," said Mom.

"There's a toy store, and a pet shop like Fur & Fangs, and an ice-cream place."

"Pirates don't play with toys," said Stink. "Or go to pet shops."

"Not even Toys *Arrr* Us?" Mom joked.

"And they definitely don't eat ice cream," said Judy.

"Not even *Marrrs Barrr* Crunch?" Dad teased.

"Sometimes parents are clueless," Judy whispered to Stink.

"We're clue-less, too," said Stink. Judy and Stink laughed till their stomachs hurt.

"Stop!" said Stink. "You're making me get scurvy again."

⚓ ⚓ ⚓

In the village, Judy and Stink saw kids with maps everywhere. "Stink. Across the street. Tall Boy and Smart Girl."

"Are you doing the Girl-Who-Cried-Pelican thing again, where you get me to look?" He looked anyway. "Let's follow them. As in spy."

"That's called cheating, Stink." said Judy.

"Pirate Rule Number Something-or-Other: Cheat every chance you get."

"*Carbunkle*," said Judy.

Judy and Stink trudged up and down Back Road and School Road behind Mom and Dad, in one shop and out the other. Stink made bored sounds. Judy made bored faces.

Until . . . they heard a voice.

"Walk the plank! Walk the plank!" said the voice. It was not a Scurvy Sam pirate voice. It was a high, squeaky voice. "Shiver me timbers! Shiver me timbers!" the voice screeched.

"I think it's coming from the pet shop," said Judy, rushing inside.

"Pet shop!" Stink called to his parents, rushing after Judy.

"Jolly Roger! Pieces of eight! Jolly Roger!"

"It's that parrot!" said Stink, pointing to a large red, yellow, and blue bird with long tail feathers. They hurried over to his cage.

"RARE!" said Judy.

"What's your name?" Stink asked in a parrot voice.

"Stink, it says right here that his name is—"

"BLACKBEARD!" Judy and Stink both screamed at the same time.

They rushed over to the teenage boy behind the counter. He had coal-black hair that fell in his eyes, a green army jacket with the sleeves ripped off, and a silver hoop earring.

"Maybe *that guy's* Blackbeard," Stink whispered.

"Do you know about the treasure hunt?" Judy asked the guy. "Because we think your parrot is Blackbeard, and that's our next clue."

51

"You got it," said the kid, putting on his red sash. He pressed a button on the cash register and handed them four pieces of eight. "That's ten!" said Stink. "We have ten! We're gonna win! We only need to solve three more clues and get six more pieces of eight."

Stink and Judy went over to the cage again. They looked around for a piece of paper inside the cage, outside the cage, under the cage. "Hey, there's nothing here," Judy said to the guy.

"He has it," the guy said, smiling. "Just ask him."

"*Bwaack!* Blackbeard singing in the dead of night!"

"Hey! He's singing that old Beatles song Dad sings about the blackbird," said Judy. "Maybe the clue's a black bird."

"Is it a black bird?" Stink asked the parrot. "Is that the clue?"

"Sign of the pirate. Sign of the pirate," said Blackbeard, ruffling his feathers and bobbing his head up and down.

"He's getting all excited. Maybe 'sign of the pirate' is the clue."

"*Bwaack!* Sign of the pirate."

"That has just got to be it," said Judy. "Every time we say the word *clue*—"

"*Bwaack!* Sign of the pirate."

"There—see what I mean?" said Judy.

"Yeah, he sounds just like a broken record," said Stink.

"Is it 'sign of the pirate'? Is that the clue?" Judy asked the guy at the counter. The guy nodded.

"Sign of the pirate," Blackbeard the parrot squawked again.

"We know! We know!" said Stink, covering his ears. "Let's get outta here. I can't think."

Judy and Stink waited outside while Mom and Dad were in the art store. A family with two little kids walked past, clutching the first clue.

"They didn't even find the You-Know-What yet," Stink whispered.

"But what about *that* kid?" said Judy. She pointed to a red-haired, freckle-faced kid with white gunk smeared on his nose. "I think I heard his pockets jingling when he walked past. As in *pirate booty.*"

Stink wasn't looking. He was busy counting silver coins again.

"Hey, Tall Boy and Smart Girl are going into the smoothie shop."

"Do you think they know something we don't know?" Stink asked.

"Not unless the shop has a pirate sign on it somewhere. C'mon, Stink. Think. Get that genius brain humming."

"Maybe they have a special flavor like Shiver Me Timbers ice cream, and that's the sign of a pirate."

"Oh, brother."

"Or else, I think it's gotta be a flag," said Stink.

"I think you have flags on the brain," said Judy.

"Yeah, on the *genius* brain," said Stink,

cracking up. "I mean a pirate flag. Every pirate has his own sign on his Jolly Roger or Bloody Red."

"Don't look now, but I think *somebody's* spying on us."

Across the street, while Smart Girl slurped a smoothie, Tall Boy was looking through binoculars—aimed right at Judy and Stink.

"Those Sneaky Petes," said Stink.

"Let 'em spy," said Judy. "We're not even doing anything."

"Yeah, they're not the only spies on this island," said Stink, taking out his spyglass and pointing it at Tall Boy. "Never mind. They're not even looking at us. Looks like they're spying on the art store."

"What's the big-whoop deal about the art store?" asked Judy. "It's just paintbrushes and stuff."

"I think they're checking out every store on this side of the street. Probably looking for any signs that have pirates on them."

Judy looked up to read the old-timey wooden sign.

"Way rare," said Judy, pointing at the sign. "Check that out. The sign is in the form of an acrostic—get it? The first letter of each word spells out *PIRATE*. That's gotta be it! I just know it! C'mon, Scurvy Stink."

Ye Artful Eye

Paintbrushes
Inks
Rubber Stamps
Art Supplies
Teacher Supplies
Easels

OPEN

Judy yanked her brother by the arm. "Let's hurry and get our next clue before those Nancy Drews beat us."

The Assistant Pirate at the art store handed over three more coins—and the next clue.

As they were leaving the store, Tall Boy and Smart Girl crossed the street, heading for the art shop. Judy and Stink ducked in a doorway and bent their heads over the next clue.

Clue
4

Nary a tick,
nary a tock—
silent, silent,
the handless clock.

Tarry no longer;
cast off all doubt.
The sands of time
are running out.

"Clock!" Stink said in a loud whisper. "It's a clock!"

"But the clue says it doesn't tick or tock," said Judy. "Or have hands. Hey, maybe it's a digital clock—like a watch."

"Let's ask Mom and Dad if there's a watch store around here."

Judy read the clue again. She looked at Stink, who was walking the plank (aka sidewalk bench), waving his pirate flag in the air while they waited for Mom and Dad to catch up.

"Hey, Stink, you know that Christopher Moody pirate guy? Didn't he have a saying about time running out?"

"That's what the hourglass stands for on his flag," said Stink. "It means don't mess with a pirate, or you'll be dead. Wait! An *hourglass* is a clock with no hands! It doesn't tick, and it doesn't tock, and it *doesn't* have hands, and it *does* have sand! The *sands* of time."

"Right you are, matey!" said Judy.

"But where are we gonna find an hour-glass?" Stink asked.

"Wherever there be dead pirates," said Judy.

I'm hot," Stink whined.

"Hi, Hot. I'm Thirsty," said Judy, cracking herself up.

"You kids have been at it all day," said Dad. "Let's go back—"

"No!" yelled Stink.

"We can get a cold drink and chill out back at the room until it's time for dinner," said Mom. "And you can look at the shells we found."

"Shells, smells," said Stink. "We can't quit now. Other People are getting close. Other People are taller than us. And smarter. Other People could win."

"For sure and absolute positive," said Judy.

They went to the antique shop. No hourglass. They checked the library. No hourglass. They went to the museum, where they saw all sorts of shipwreck stuff—but no hourglass.

"What a bust," said Judy.

"At least we got to see real gold," said Stink.

"You mean gold *dust*," said Judy. "C'mon, Stinkerbell. We've been looking for an hourglass for the last *hour*. Even I want to go back."

"Okay, Poopy Longstocking," said Stink.

68

⚓ ⚓ ⚓

Back at the inn, Stink flopped on the big bed and stared at the ceiling.

"*Now* who's Poopy Longstocking?" said Judy.

"Yeah, but she had a suitcase full of gold coins," said Stink. "We got nothing. *Nada.* Zip. Zero."

"Don't give up the ship now," said Judy. "We only need three more."

"After a rest," said Mom, "how about if we get some dinner, then go on the town Ghost Walk? I got some art supplies in case you want to make rubbings of any of the old gravestones."

Stink sat up. "Will there be dead pirates?"

At the first sign of dusk, a group of visitors met in the parking lot outside the Village Artisan.

"Guess who's following us? I mean, *spying* on us. Tall Boy and Smart Girl! Copycats," Stink hissed.

"Copy kittens," Judy echoed.

A white-haired man with a bolo tie led the tour. "Almost three hundred years ago, Blackbeard met his death here. They went *chop*—off with his head—then tossed him overboard. Story goes, the headless body swam around the ship seven times before going under." He pointed through the trees to a sandy beach. "Some say if you go out on Springer's Point at night, you'll see the ghost of Blackbeard himself, glowing in the dark, roaming around, looking for that head."

The small band of people followed the man up and down Howard Street, peering over wooden fences into graveyards, where they were treated to stories of folks buried on the island: Old Diver; Edgar the banjo player. They stopped at three cemeteries sprinkled with headstones that had ships and seashells, anchors and arrows, hearts and handshakes.

But not one single hourglass.

At the end of the tour, they came to a small graveyard behind a big white historic house that was now a museum.

Judy was working on a gravestone rubbing of a whale when Stink rushed up to her. "Guess what? I was spying on the You-Know-Whos. I heard Tall Boy say '*X* marks the spot.' Then they both died laughing, like it was a really good joke."

"Weird," said Judy.

"Double weird," Stink agreed. "So I followed them."

"Did you find out anything about an hourglass?" Judy whispered.

"Did I!" Stink pulled out a rolled-up piece of paper from behind his back. When he unrolled it, Judy saw a crayon rubbing of an old pirate grave with an hourglass on it. The shape of the hourglass looked like a big *X*.

"*X does* mark the spot," said Judy. "This has to be it, Stink. I feel it in my bones. Let's go turn it in and get our silver."

Judy and Stink ran around to the front of the house and yanked on the door. It was closed. As in *not open.* As in *locked up tight.*

Stink pressed his nose to the glass, peering in the front window. "We have to bust in there, or Tall Boy and Smart Girl are gonna beat us for sure."

"Stink, it's too late. Nobody's here. We can't just bust in —"

"Hey, maybe we could set off the fire alarm!"

"Great idea, Stink — if you want to go to jail."

"Wish that I had super-duper, double-quadruple X-ray vision," said Stink. "If there's another clue, I'd see it from here."

"Forget it, Stink. We just have to wait till morning."

"Says you," said Stink.

"Says Pirate Rule Number Ten-and-a-Half: He who breaks into a museum after dark will get locked in the brig, fed to the scurvy rats, and end up in Davy Jones's Locker. Mad Molly O'Maggot has spoken."

"Drat and bilge bunkle!" said Stink.

As Judy and Stink went back down the steps, a blood-red moon rose in the sky. Twisty branches of the live oaks made spooky shadows across the sidewalk. An owl hooted. Tree frogs croaked. Judy and Stink nearly jumped out of their skins when they heard a squeaky, creaking sound.

"It's just this rusty old gate, folks," said the tour guide. "Or is it? Folks around these parts have been known to hear

strange sounds: laughs, cries, voices out of nowhere. Flashes of light that can't be explained."

Stink shivered. Judy pulled her arms up into her sweatshirt.

"Let's get outta here," said Stink. "This place gives me the spooks."

"Some pirate," said Judy.

⚓ ⚓ ⚓

When Judy and Stink finally fell asleep that night, visions of hourglasses danced in their heads.

The next morning, they dragged Dad out of bed as soon as they woke up. As he drove them to the old white house, Judy kept an eye out for Tall Boy and Smart Girl.

Stink checked Dad's watch a hundred times. At last, a lady with ten hundred keys came to open the door. "You're up early," said the lady. "You must be treasure hunters."

"Sure are," said Dad. "Have you had many others?"

"Like maybe possibly a real tall boy?" said Stink. "And a girl who wears glasses and looks super-smart?"

"You're my first customers," said the lady.

Stink unrolled his rubbing of the gravestone with the hourglass and showed it to the lady with the red sash. "Is this it? Did we figure it out? Do we get any silver?"

"Yes, yes, and yes," said the lady, handing over two silver pieces.

Stink dumped out all his coins on the counter. "Two, four, six . . . fifteen! All we need is one more. One!"

"Okay, Stink. I can count," said Judy. "But we still have to figure out the last and final clue, and it's the hardest. We only have till twelve noon."

"Here you go," said the lady, handing the clue to Judy.

"Let's go back to the inn and get Mom. Then we can all go eat some breakfast," said Dad.

"I'm not hungry," said Stink. "Read it! Read it!" he cried. Judy read the clue:

Clue 5

Sound without ears,
voice without tongue,
rings without fingers,
song without lung.

Hear the sound;
get the lay of the land.
Find the last silver
at the crab's right hand.

"Spitballs and barnacles," said Stink. "It doesn't make sense. Sound, but no ears? A voice, but no tongue? Not possible."

"Other stuff has a tongue," said Judy. "Like sneakers."

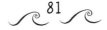

"But sneakers don't have a voice," Stink pointed out.

"Well—bells have rings, but they don't have fingers."

"Great. All we have to do is find a giant talking sneaker bell."

"Or in your case, a Stinker Bell." Judy cracked herself up.

"What about the crab's right hand?" Stink asked. "It says, 'Find the last silver at the crab's right hand.' Crabs don't even have hands."

"A crab's right hand is a claw, Stink. A crab claw."

"There are millions of crabs on this island, and they all have claws."

"But there's only one place called the Crab's Claw," said Judy, pointing to the map. "It's a restaurant on Ocean View Road."

"Suddenly I'm hungry," said Stink. "Hungry as a shark."

Before Judy and Stink could step inside the Crab's Claw, out came another family. Tall Boy and Smart Girl! Judy said, "Hi."

"Why did you say hi?" Stink asked when they sat down.

"It just popped out," said Judy.

"Tall Boy and *Crab* Girl are beating our pants off. Did they look like they were just eating breakfast? Or searching for clues? What if they already found the gold and we're too late?"

"Chill out, Curious George," said Judy. "Believe me, if they found it, we'd know." Judy dug through all the sugar packets at the table and found four with seashells for her collection.

"Let's look for the last piece of eight," Stink urged. "Scurvy Sam said it would be hard. But it has to be here—it just has to."

"Order first," said Mom.

Stink stared at the menu.

Menu

Crab Omelette
Crab Suzette
Crab & Eggs Benedict
Crab Fritters
Blue Crab Bagel
She-Crab Casserole

"This menu sure is crabby."

"*You* sure are crabby," said Judy.

"You're crabbier," said Stink.

"You're crabbiest," said Judy.

"You're a she-crab," said Stink.

"Well, you're a he-crab," said Judy.

The waiter asked, "What can I get for you folks this morning?"

"A glass of water, please," said Stink.

"Me, too," said Judy.

"Kids," said Mom, "you have to eat."

"Order cereal," Judy told Stink. "That's the fastest."

While they waited for their food, Judy and Stink nosed around, searching for the last coin hidden in a crab's claw. There were crabs hanging in nets on the walls.

There were crabby curtains, crab-shaped mirrors, crab door knockers.

"There are ten hundred million crabs in this place," said Judy.

But not one single piece of silver.

"I got it!" said Stink. "One time I saw this old movie called *Mysterious Island,* and these two guys, Ted and Ned or something, walk *right on top* of this evil giant crab under the sand. The crab attacks and grabs Ned—"

"How do you know it was Ned?"

"I'm just saying," said Stink. "Anyway, listen. Ned screams while the other guy ties a rope around one of the giant crab's claws. He flips the crab off a cliff and tosses him into a pool of super-boiling-

hot water. And then they eat him."

"Food's here," Dad called to them.

"So what's your point?" Judy asked.

"My point is that there could be a giant crab hidden under the sand on this island, and in his right claw could be the silver coin. Why didn't I think of it before?"

"Go figure," said Judy.

⚓ ⚓ ⚓

On their way out, Stink asked, "Is this the right hand of the crab?"

"No, it's the Crab's Claw," said the lady behind the counter.

"Are you by any chance an Assistant Pirate? Do you have a silver piece of eight hidden somewhere?"

"Not here, I'm afraid," said the lady,

shaking her head. "Sorry, kids."

"So what's next?" Dad asked when they got outside.

"Oops, I have to go back," said Judy. "I forgot my sugar packets. And my place mat. I want to save it for my scrapbook."

"Hurry up!" said Stink. "We're almost out of time."

A few minutes later, Judy came rushing out of the restaurant, waving her place mat in the air. "Stink! I think I found it. Take a look at this." She held out her paper place mat for Stink to see.

"So? It's a place mat," said Stink.

"Look at what's *on* the place mat," said Judy.

Stink looked again. "So? It's a map."

Judy pointed again. "Stop being a Crabby Appleton for one second and look harder."

"So? It's a map of the island."

"It's a map of the island *and* the Atlantic Ocean *and* Pamlico Sound." Judy traced her finger around the tip of land that formed Silver Lake Harbor. "Look at the shape of the island."

"So? It looks like—" Finally it hit him. "It looks like a giant crab claw!" Stink shrieked, jumping up and down.

Judy clamped a hand over his mouth. "Tell the whole world, why don't you?"

Dad turned onto Silver Lake Drive, and they followed it around the harbor.

"Take us out as far as you can go, Dad," said Stink.

"Yeah, to the tip of the crab's claw," said Judy.

"We can park at the Visitor Center," Mom suggested.

They got out of the car and looked around. "I see a bunch of kids with maps," Mom said. "They seem to be crossing the boardwalk over to the museum. But the tip of the island is really the old Coast Guard station. It's the one with the bell out front, down by the water."

"Bell?" said Judy and Stink at the same time.

"A bell rings," said Stink, "but doesn't have fingers."

"What do you call that thingie that hangs inside a bell?"

"A clapper," said Mom.

"Or a tongue," said Dad.

"'Sound without ears,'" said Stink.

"'Voice without tongue,'" said Judy. "I bet that bell doesn't ring."

"'Cause there's pirate booty in there." Stink stopped in his tracks. "I think I just saw Tall Boy and Smart Girl go into the museum. What if there's another bell in there? The right one?"

But Judy had already taken off. "Wait for me!" cried Stink.

They stopped in front of a large brass bell, like the Liberty Bell but without the crack. Stink pushed it. "It doesn't ring!"

"But look inside! Look inside!" Judy squealed. Stink stuck his head up inside the bell. "See anything?"

"Dark," said Stink. "Flashlight!"

Judy dug into Stink's backpack and pulled out the flashlight. She stuck her head inside the bell and shone the flashlight all around.

Suddenly, the beam of light hit something shiny. A shimmer. A sparkle. Silver! A shiny silver coin was duct-taped to the inside of the bell.

"Eureka!" said Judy.

"Mom! Dad!" yelled Stink. "We struck gold!"

"Well, really, we struck silver," said Judy. "But that means we win, win, win!" Judy and Stink screamed and hugged each other. People nearby stared, squirrels skittered, and seagulls took flight.

Judy and Stink jumped around and shouted until they were all out of breath, and collapsed in a fit of giggles. Stink got the hiccups because he laughed so hard. "I feel—*hic*—like I won—*hic*—the Olympics!" said Stink. *"HIC!"*

"The Hiccup Olympics," said Judy.

A guy from the Coast Guard station came up and shook hands with them. "Base to Scurvy Sam," he said into a walkie-talkie. "Come in, Scurvy Sam. We have a couple of winners."

Mom and Dad caught up and peered at the silver coin. "I can't believe we beat Tall Boy and Smart Girl," said Stink. "Just in time, too."

"I like how you kids stuck it out and didn't give up," said Dad.

"See what can happen when you two work together?" said Mom.

"Two brains are better than one," said Judy.

"Especially when it's Scurvy-Stink-and-Mad-Molly-O'Maggot brains," Stink said, tapping his head.

⚓ ⚓ ⚓

Scurvy Stink and Mad Molly reported to Pirate Headquarters just before twelve noon. A small crowd of people had gathered, waiting.

Stink and Judy ran up to Scurvy Sam. Stink opened his pouch and counted out all sixteen pieces of eight. Scurvy Sam's eyes lit up brighter than the firecrackers that Blackbeard was famous for having in his beard. "Well, blow me down. If it ain't Mad Molly and Scurvy Stink. Ain't you two o' the smartest urchins on the Outer Banks!"

Scurvy Sam climbed aboard his ship and clanged the bell twelve times. "Avast, me hearties! We have us two winners!" After a big speech, Scurvy Sam climbed down and went up to Judy and Stink. He raised their hands in the air, then danced a funny hornpipe. The crowd clapped and hooted.

"Now tell us, fer all to hear," he said.

"How'd ye do it, me mateys? What's yer secret? *Arrr.*"

"Just super-duper brain power," said Stink, tapping his head. "And a trusty-dusty survival kit."

"And a little luck," Judy said. "Even though Stink almost got us in jail." The crowd broke into laughter.

Scurvy Sam presented Judy and Stink each with a shiny gold doubloon. Stink's had a skull and crossbones and said *1587* on the back.

"Rare," said Judy. "Mine has pictures of Blackbeard *and* Anne Bonny!"

"Whoa, it's like a *gold* silver dollar," said Stink. "Is it real?"

Arrr!

"It'll break yer teeth if ye bite it."

"It's not cursed, is it?" Stink asked.

Scurvy Sam winked. "Would an old sea dog like me curse a fellow pirate?" He turned back to the crowd.

"That be it, mateys. Thanks be to ye one and all for makin' the Third Annual Pirate Treasure Hunt such a dandy hoot and a holler. Now, mind ye, don't be leavin' without yer pirate booty! Treasure for all!" The Assistant Pirates passed out goody bags while Scurvy Sam shook hands and waved good-bye to all the treasure hunters.

"I told you it was the bell," said a Girl voice.

"I know you did, but you never said

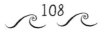

which bell, and there was one inside the museum!" said a Boy voice.

Judy's eyes grew wide. Stink hiccupped. Tall Boy and Smart Girl!

"You're so lucky," Smart Girl said to Judy and Stink. "We came all the way from Maine, and we really wanted to win."

"We tried way hard. We were sure we had it," said Tall Boy.

"Wow!" said Smart Girl, eyeing Stink's doubloon. "Sure is shiny."

"Yeah," said Stink. "There's only one thing better than gold."

"What could be better than gold?" Judy asked.

"A ride on a for-real pirate ship!" said Stink.

"I'd give anything to ride on a pirate ship," said Tall Boy.

Judy looked at Stink. Stink looked at Judy. She couldn't help feeling funny about beating them. She could tell Stink felt bad, too.

"Actually, we can't go for a ride on the pirate ship after all," Judy said.

"What!?" said Smart Girl and Tall Boy at the same time.

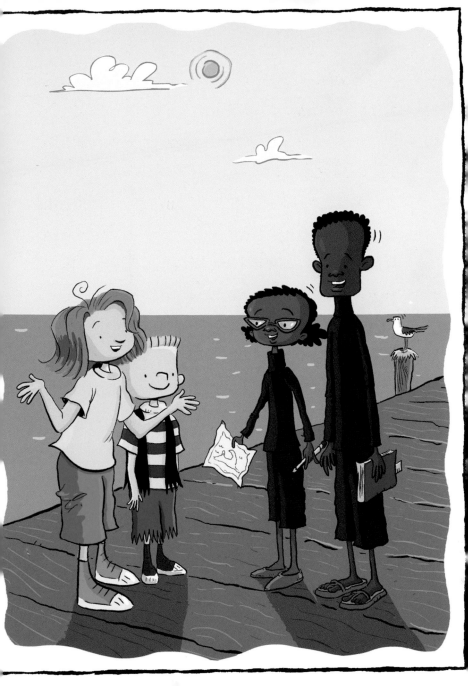

"Have ye lost yer senses?" said Scurvy Sam, overhearing them.

"Not alone, anyway. We'd be breaking Pirate Rule Number Two," said Judy.

"That's right!" Stink piped in. "Pirate Rule Two says that if you find treasure, you have to share it—even-steven."

"By jiggers, they be right!" said Scurvy Sam. "And the punishment for breakin' Pirate Rule Number Two be marooning ye on a desert island with nothin' but bugs for grub."

"You gotta come with us," Stink told Tall Boy and Smart Girl.

"Save us from eating bugs," said Judy.

"Besides," said Stink, "you guys kinda helped us win."

"We did?" asked Smart Girl, crinkling her nose.

"We saw you guys looking through your binoculars, so we looked, too. That's how we found the sign of the pirate."

"But we found it 'cause of *you*," said Tall Boy. "We saw you pointing up at the sign in front of the art shop, and that made us look."

"But Stink heard *you* saying '*X* marks the spot' at the graveyard, so he followed you," Judy said. "That's how we found the hourglass."

Smart Girl looked at Scurvy Sam. "Can we?"

"I'd be mighty honored to have two more pirates aboard, me beauty."

113

"You mean it?" asked Smart Girl.

"I swear it, in the name of Davy Jones."

"Okay, you can come," said Stink. "But only on one condition."

"What's that?" asked Tall Boy.

"You have to clean the poop deck!" said Stink.

"Arrgh!" moaned Tall Boy and Smart Girl.

"Kidding!" Stink said, and everybody cracked up. Stink laughed the loudest— a laugh that could be heard on the wind, across the seven seas, and back again . . . a laugh that was sure to haunt Pirate Island for years to come.

PIRATE RULES

1. Every crew member has an equal vote and a equal share of food and drink on ship.

2. All crew members have an equal share i treasure.

3. There is to be no playing cards or dice fo money.

4. Lights and candles shall be out by eight o'cloc each night, or else!

5. Every crew member must have a pistol and cutlass ready for use at all times.

6. No girl or woman shall be allowed on board ship. Break this rule and die!

7. Deserting ship in battle shall result in death or marooning.

8. There is no fighting allowed on board ship. All quarrels must be settled on shore.

9. There is to be no talk of jumping ship until everyone has shared at least one thousand pounds.

10. The ship's musician shall rest on Sundays.

Another laugh-out-loud adventure with
Judy Moody and Stink!

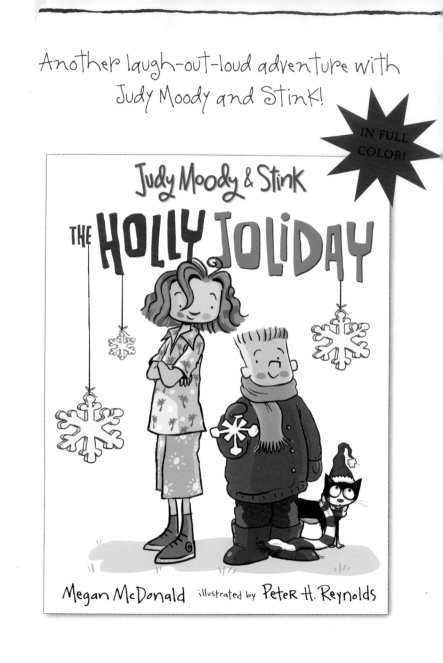

IN FULL
COLOR!

Judy Moody & Stink

THE HOLLY JOLIDAY

Megan McDonald   illustrated by PeteR H. Reynolds